The Big Race

Written by Morgan Matthews
Illustrated by S.D. Schindler

Troll Associates

Library of Congress Cataloging-in-Publication Data

Matthews, Morgan.
  The big race.

  (Fiddlesticks)
  Summary: Tired of losing every event in the
animals' annual sports contest, Manny Moose decides
to concentrate his efforts on training for just one
event, the cross-country race.
  [1. Winning and losing—Fiction. 2. Racing—Fiction.
3. Moose—Fiction. 4. Animals—Fiction]
I. Schindler, S. D., ill. II. Title. III. Series.
PZ7.M43425Bi 1989   [E]   88-1287
ISBN 0-8167-1329-4 (lib. bdg.)
ISBN 0-8167-1330-8 (pbk.)

Summer was an exciting time in the
forest. It was then that the animals held
their yearly sports contest—the Great Games.

The Great Games were very special.
Animals came from near and far to take part
in them. Burly bears lumbered down from
the mountains. Fleet jack rabbits left their
grassy meadows. Out of the forest came
squirrels, raccoons, and animals of all shapes
and sizes.

One by one, everyone came to take part in the Great Games.

The sports contest had many events. There were different kinds of races. There were tests of strength, like the shot-put. There were jumping, swimming, and other sports, too.

All of the animals tried hard to win.
Beavers and otters swam their fastest. Quick
foxes ran their swiftest. White-tailed hares
jumped their highest.

Why? Because the player who turned in
the most outstanding performance became
champion of the forest for a year. And to be
named champion of the forest was the
greatest honor of all.

"Champion of the forest," sighed Manny
Moose, as he walked through the woods.
"Manny the Champion. I like the sound of
that."

Manny Moose smiled and dreamed about
winning at the Great Games.

But Manny really wasn't much of a player. He wasn't strong. And he couldn't jump high or run fast. To tell the truth, the moose was a bit clumsy. He was always tripping, slipping, or stumbling.

Because Manny was so clumsy, some of the other animals made fun of him. Manny didn't like that at all. He wanted to prove he could be a winner, too.

"I'll run races," said Manny. "I'll swim. I'll jump. I'll show everyone I'm not a clumsy moose." Manny was so busy daydreaming, he didn't watch where he was going.

He tripped over a tree root. *Thump!* Hooves over horns he went. "Whoops!" he yelled as he tumbled.

Over and over he rolled. Down a hill he went. At the bottom of the slope he bumped into a tree stump. *Thump!*

The stump happened to be at the gates of the Great Games. Other animals there began to laugh at Manny.

"What's this? A funny-looking boulder?" teased Bruce Bear.

"It's furry and has horns like a moose," chuckled Harry Hare.

Up walked Coach Owl. He was in charge of the games. "Are you all right?" the coach asked, as he helped Manny to his feet.

Manny rubbed the big lump that had swelled up between his antlers. "I'm fine," he replied. "Am I too late to be in the games?"

THE GREAT GAMES

"Did you hear that?" said Franny Fox.
Franny was one of the fastest runners in the
forest. "Manny wants to be in the Great
Games."

"Maybe he thinks there is a clumsy
contest," chuckled Bruce Bear. Bruce was
very big and strong.

10

"I'm not joking," replied Manny. "I want to be in the games." He looked at Coach Owl. "Can I?"

Slowly, Coach Owl nodded. "Yes," he replied. "What sport did you practice for?"

Manny made a silly face. "Well," he admitted, "I didn't practice for any. But I'll find an easy one I can win."

A short time later the games began. Manny decided to try the shot-put. Throwing a round metal ball didn't look too hard. But Manny didn't know how heavy that ball was.

Big Bruce Bear went first. He picked up the heavy ball to his shoulder. Then he tossed it with all of his might. *Whoosh!* Through the air it flew. It went very far.

"Very good, Bruce," said Coach Owl.

Manny was next. He bent over to pick up
the ball. Was it ever heavy! He groaned as
he slowly lifted it off of the ground.

"I . . . I can't hold it," Manny sputtered.
He let go of the ball. *Klunk!* It fell right on
his toe.

"Ouch!" he screamed, hopping on one
toe.

It was quite a sight!

Manny decided the shot-put was not as easy as it looked. Next, he tried the diving contest. He watched Otto Otter dive gracefully into the water.

"I can do that," said Manny, as he climbed up the diving board.

The diving board was wet and slick. Manny took one step and slipped. "Oh no! Not again," he cried.

Splash!

Manny did the biggest bellywhopper ever seen. Everyone laughed at the sight of the clumsy moose.

But Manny did not give up. He tried to
race against Franny Fox. She was fast.
Manny was slow. Franny won the race
before Manny took three steps.

The jumping contest was not easy for
Manny either. Everyone clapped when Harry
Hare jumped. They did *not* cheer when
Manny tried to jump and fell flat on his face.

Poor Manny Moose couldn't do anything
right. He stumbled his way through one
game after another.

At long last, Coach Owl had a talk with
Manny. "I don't think you should take part
in any more of the games," the coach said.

Manny felt hurt. "I wanted to win at
something just once," he said. "I wanted to
know what it feels like to be a winner."

Coach Owl nodded. "I think you *can* be a winner," answered the coach. "You may be clumsy, but you have one thing a winner needs."

Manny's face brightened. "What is that?"

"Determination," replied Coach Owl. "A true winner never gives up." He paused a minute. "But you are trying to become a winner in the wrong way."

Manny was confused. "What do you mean?" he asked.

Coach Owl explained, "You can't become a winner by going from one thing to another, looking for an easy way to win."

"What should I do then?" asked Manny.

"Find a game you like and put all your energy into it," said Coach Owl. "Practice that sport until you are very good at it. And I know just the race for you."

"You do?" Manny exclaimed. "Which one?"

Coach Owl walked away. "Follow me," he said. He led Manny to where a special race was about to begin. It was called the Big Race. The race went over hills, through the woods, and around the mountain.

"This is the biggest race of all," said Coach Owl. "It's a long, hard race over many miles. To win the Big Race, a runner needs determination."

Bang! A gun sounded. The Big Race began. Manny watched as the runners started into the woods.

In silence, the moose waited while the long race was run. Hours later, a tired Rob Rabbit crossed the finish line to win the race.

It was then that Manny turned to Coach Owl and spoke. "I would like to try this race," he said. "What do I have to do?"

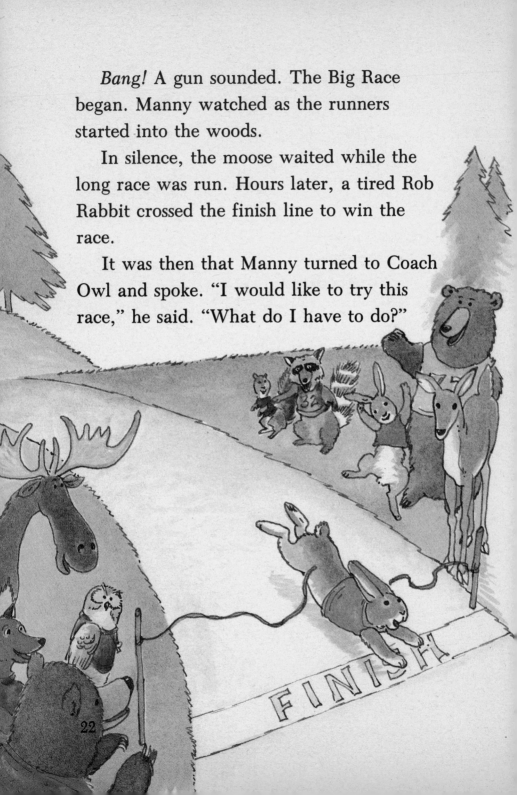

Coach Owl looked at Manny. "Practice!
Practice! Practice!" he replied. "If you work
hard and run every day, you will be ready
for the Big Race next year."

"I will be ready," Manny promised.

"Good," said Coach Owl. "I'll write
down some ideas for you to follow when you
practice."

The next day, Manny Moose began practicing. He followed the suggestions Coach Owl gave him. He stretched his muscles before running and wore the proper clothes. Then off he went.

It was a beautiful day, and the birds were singing. "This is more like fun than work," Manny said as he ran along at a steady pace.

Manny ran around the pine forest and then home. He took his time and stopped when he felt tired. He didn't run too far or too fast. When he was done, he felt tired but good.

As time passed, Manny got stronger and
ran farther. Of course, he was still a bit
clumsy. Once while running around the lake,
he slipped and fell in. Another time he
started to daydream and bumped into a tree
branch.

But the more he ran, the less clumsy he
seemed to be. Most important of all, Manny
liked what he was doing and felt good about
doing it.

Manny kept on running as the seasons changed. It wasn't always fun. Some days it was really hard work.

"I don't feel like running today," said Manny. He looked out of his cozy house and saw snow on the ground. "But I'll do it anyway. To be a winner, you have to keep trying. And I want to win."

Finally, by summer, Manny could run the full distance of the Big Race. He wasn't clumsy anymore. In fact, he felt like a champion.

"Now, at long last, I'm ready for the Big Race," said Manny. And ready he was!

"Welcome back," said Coach Owl when
Manny arrived at the Great Games. "Have
you been practicing?"

"Yes," Manny replied. "I'm ready to run
in the Big Race."

"Good," said Coach Owl. "Follow me.
The race is about to begin."

When the other runners saw Manny, they laughed.

"Beating Manny will be easy," Chester Chipmunk chuckled.

Rob Rabbit, last year's champion, didn't even give Manny a second thought. Neither did most of the other runners. They didn't know about the new Manny.

Bang! The race began.

Much to everyone's surprise, Manny didn't stumble at the start. He ran along taking graceful strides. At the first turn in the forest he was still with the others.

When the runners came out of the woods, Rob Rabbit broke away from the others. One by one, the runners followed. Chester Chipmunk and Manny were left to bring up the rear.

"I don't like this," gasped Chester. "That moose is right behind me." Chester was worried. He did not want to be passed by a silly moose. Chester kept looking back at Manny. He should have been looking ahead. *Crash!* He bumped right into a tree.

Manny stopped. "Are you all right?" he
asked Chester.

Chester rubbed his aching head and
nodded. Away ran Manny Moose. There
were many miles to go. The race was far
from over.

Manny ran and ran. He didn't think
about winning. He just tried to do the best
he could do.

Soon he saw Bill Badger sitting on a rock.
Bill had dropped out of the race. He looked
exhausted.

"I tried to go too far too fast," Bill puffed
as Manny passed. "I can't run anymore."

The warm summer sun heated up as the race continued. It made running difficult. But Manny did not slow down. He passed runner after runner.

Finally, near the lake, he caught up with Randy Raccoon.

"The race is half over," Randy sighed. "But it's too hot to run anymore."

Manny didn't reply. He just took step after step.

"Finishing this race isn't important," Randy said. "I'm going swimming instead." He stopped running and jumped into the cool lake.

"I started this race," said Manny, "and I'm going to finish it. I may not win. But I am not a quitter."

Away he went, leaving Randy to splash in the lake.

A bit later Manny saw Willie Weasel.
Soon the two were running side by side.

"How many runners are ahead of us?"
asked Manny as he took a deep breath.

"Only one," Willie replied. "It's Rob
Rabbit, and he has a big lead."

On and on they ran. At the top of a hill they spied Rob Rabbit far ahead.

"We'll never catch him," said the weasel. "But I know a secret short cut. If we take it, we can pass him."

Manny gave Willie a dirty look. "That's cheating," he scolded. "Winning only counts if you do it fair and square."

Manny ran faster. He left Willie far behind.

"You'll be sorry," Willie shouted, as he turned onto his short cut. But the short cut was no good. The path was muddy.

Splat! Into a mud puddle he fell. The race was over for him.

Meanwhile, Manny kept up a quick pace.
All of his hard work was paying off. Slowly
but surely, he was catching up to Rob
Rabbit.

Manny ran. Suddenly, he was right behind Rob. "Faster," Manny gasped. "I have to run faster."

Stride by stride, Manny Moose moved ahead. Before long, Rob and Manny were neck and neck.

Ahead was the finish line. Both runners moved as quickly as they could. Faster, faster, faster went Rob Rabbit. Faster, faster, faster ran Manny Moose. Never before had anyone seen such a finish to the Big Race. Who would win?

With one final burst of speed, Manny
moved ahead. By a nose, he crossed the
finish line in front of Rob Rabbit.

"Manny Moose wins!" said Coach Owl.
"Manny wins the race!"

The crowd clapped and cheered.

For the first time in his life, Manny was a winner! It was a great feeling.

Manny went up to Rob Rabbit. "You ran a great race," he said.

Rob smiled. "You did, too," he replied. "And you deserved to win."

"Manny Moose—he's the champion of the forest," shouted Franny Fox.

"Yes," called Bruce Bear. "Manny's our champ!"

Rob Rabbit and Harry Hare agreed. Soon all of the animals were cheering Manny as the champion of the forest.

"You did it," said the coach to the moose.
Manny smiled proudly. "Even a clumsy
moose can be a winner if he believes in
himself and works hard," Manny said.
And that's how Manny Moose won the
Big Race and became champion of the forest.